10 LITTLE KITTENS

Retold by MEGAN BORGERT-SPANIOL

Illustrated by MAXINE LEE

CANTATA
LEARNING
MANKATO, MINNESOTA

CANTATA LEARNING

MANKATO, MINNESOTA

Published by Cantata Learning
1710 Roe Crest Drive
North Mankato, MN 56003
www.cantatalearning.com

Library of Congress Control Number: 2014938337
ISBN: 978-1-63290-068-5

10 Little Kittens retold by Megan Borgert-Spaniol
Illustrated by Maxine Lee

Book design by Tim Palin Creative
Music produced by Wes Schuck
Audio recorded, mixed, and mastered at Two Fish Studios, Mankato, MN

Printed in the United States of America.

VISIT

WWW.CANTATALEARNING.COM/ACCESS-OUR-MUSIC

Baby animals like to stay together. Kittens and puppies cuddle and play. **Piglets** eat from a **trough**, and **chicks** follow the leader. Count to 10 and back to 1 with these happy little friends!

When you hear the baby animal, turn the page.

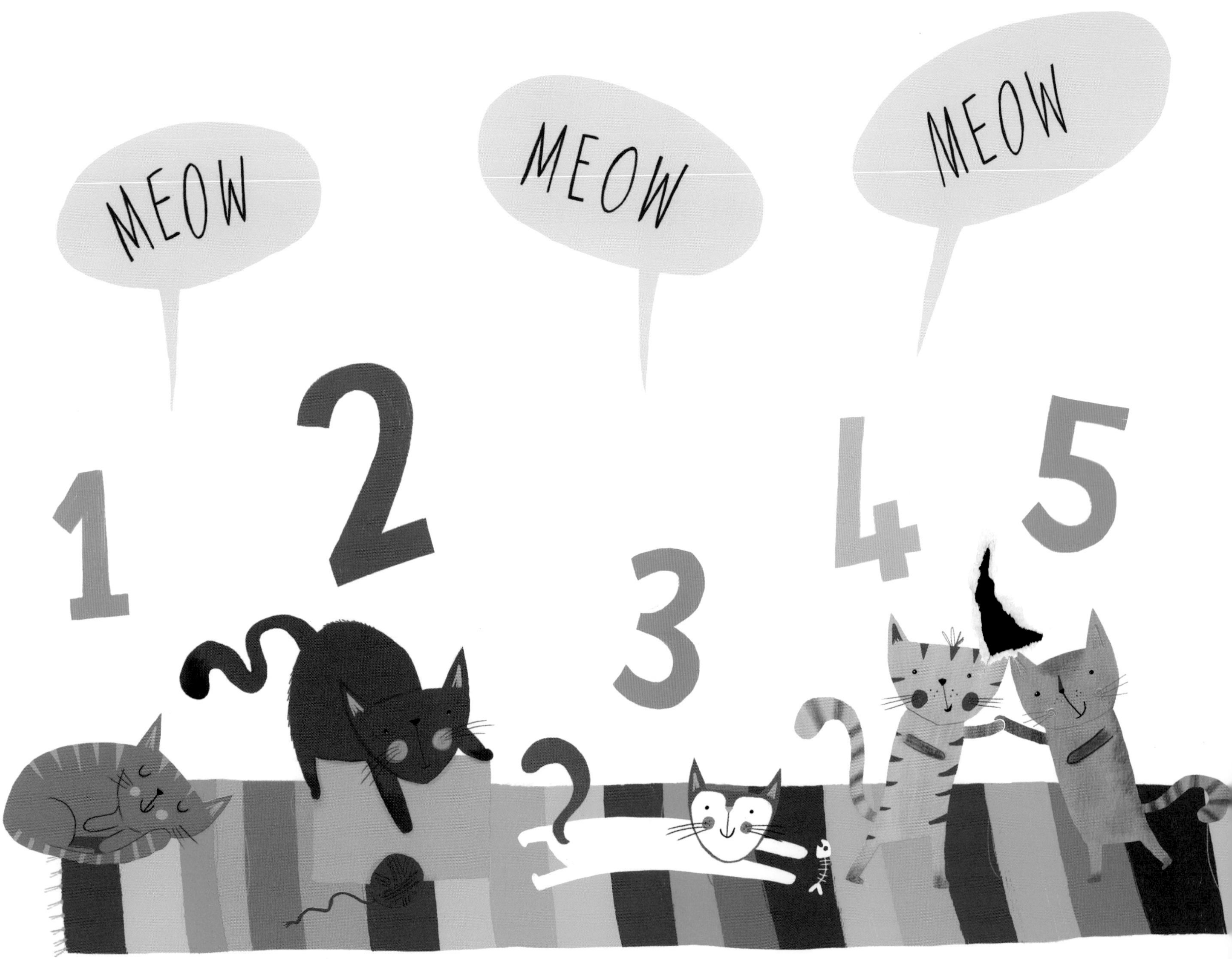
MEOW
MEOW
MEOW
1
2
3
4
5

1 little, 2 little, 3 little kittens,
4 little, 5 little, 6 little kittens,
7 little, 8 little, 9 little kittens,
10 little kittens say, "Meow, meow, meow."

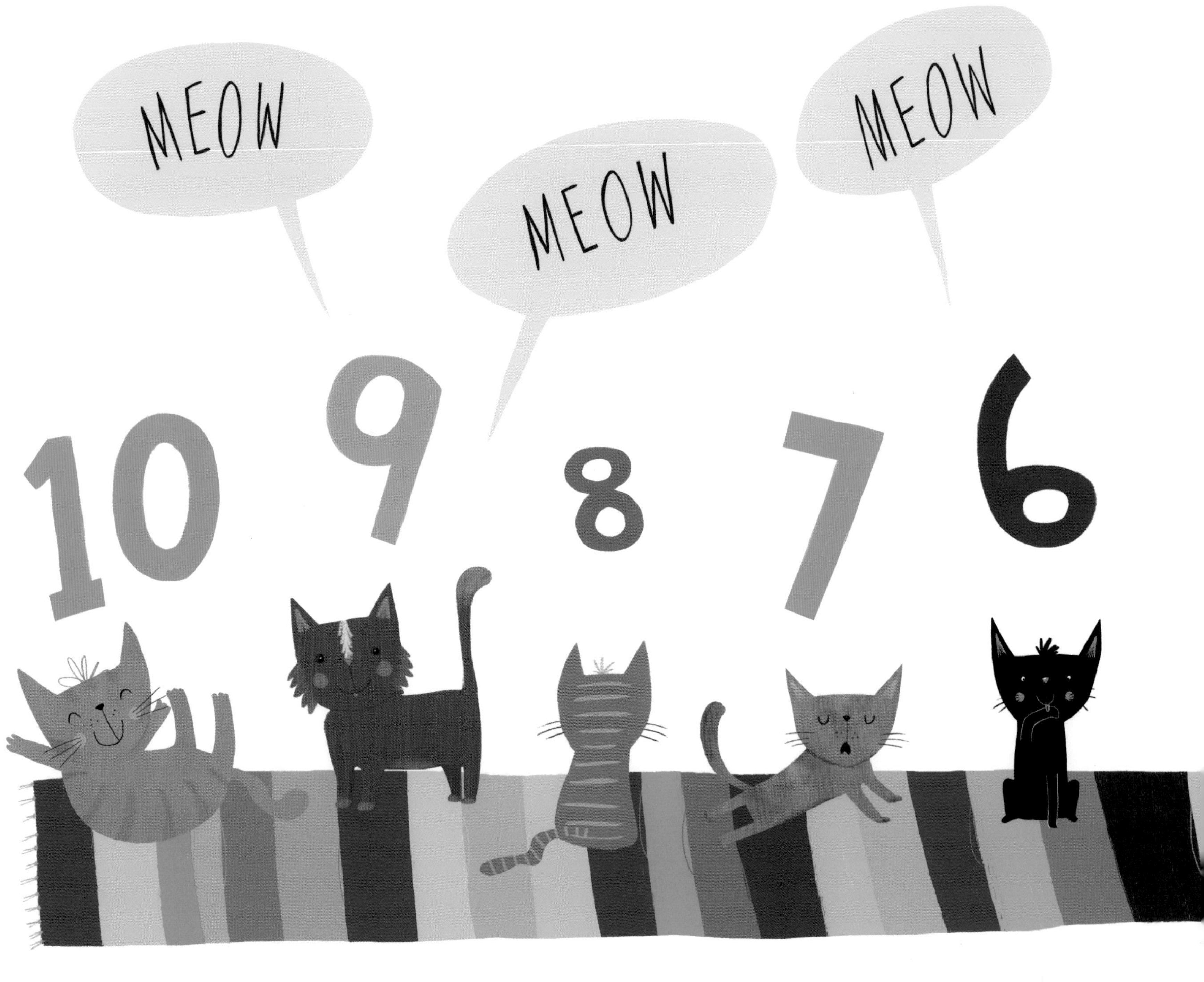
MEOW
MEOW
MEOW
10 9 8 7 6

10 little, 9 little, 8 little kittens,
7 little, 6 little, 5 little kittens,
4 little, 3 little, 2 little kittens,
1 little kitten says, "Meow, meow, meow."

10

1 little, 2 little, 3 little piggies,
4 little, 5 little, 6 little piggies,
7 little, 8 little, 9 little piggies,
10 little piggies say, "Oink, oink, oink."

10 little, 9 little, 8 little piggies,
7 little, 6 little, 5 little piggies,
4 little, 3 little, 2 little piggies,
1 little piggy says, "Oink, oink, oink."

PEEP!

PEEP!

PEEP!

1 2 3 4 5

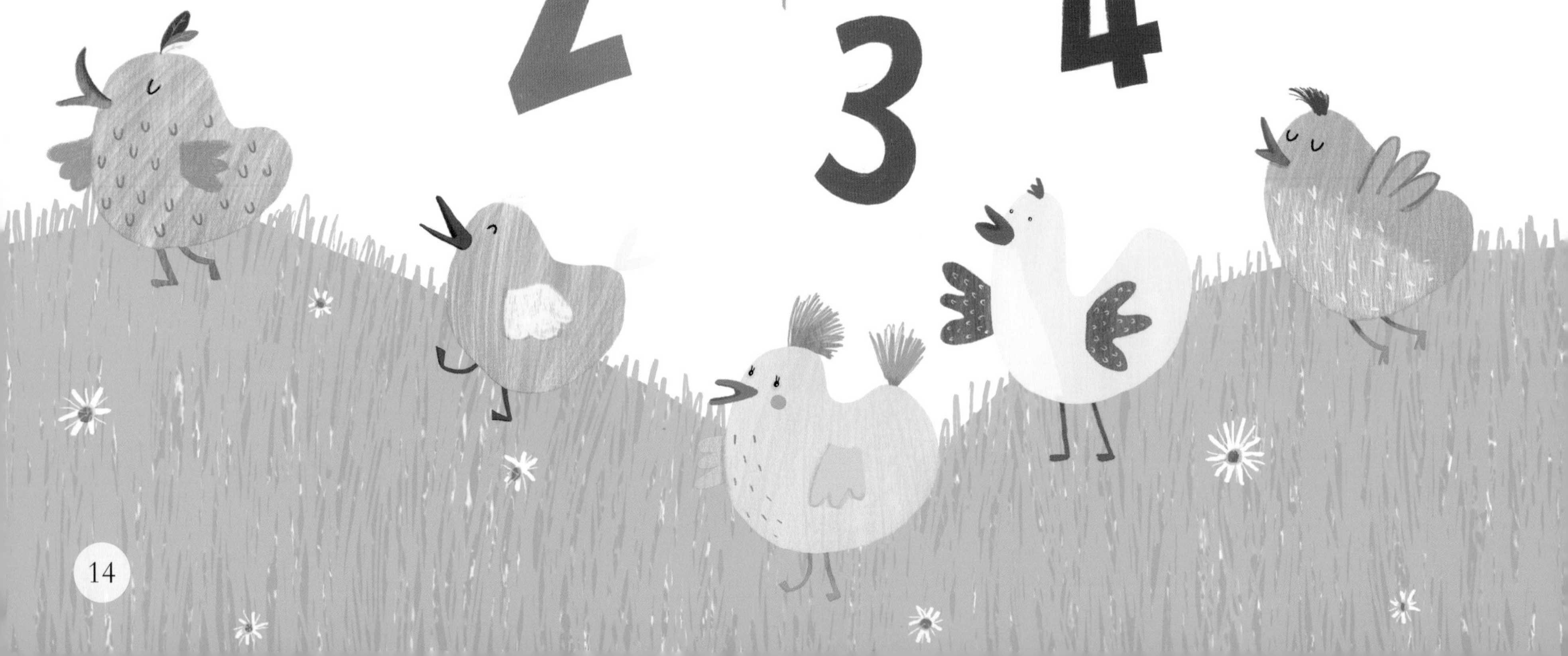

1 little, 2 little, 3 little chicks,
4 little, 5 little, 6 little chicks,
7 little, 8 little, 9 little chicks,
10 little chicks say, "Peep, peep, peep."

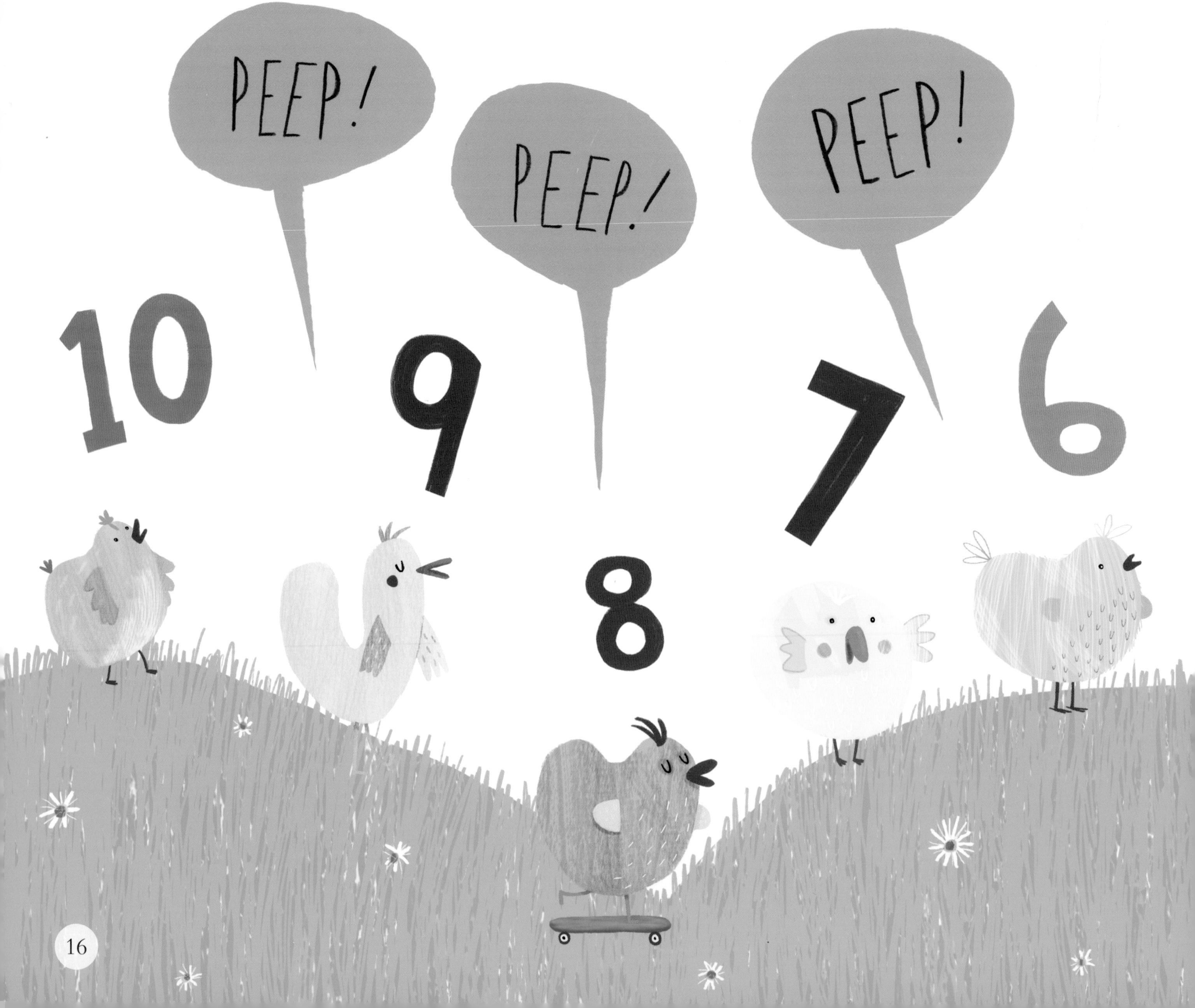
PEEP!
PEEP!
PEEP!
10
9
8
7
6

10 little, 9 little, 8 little chicks,
7 little, 6 little, 5 little chicks,
4 little, 3 little, 2 little chicks,
1 little chick says, "Peep, peep, peep."

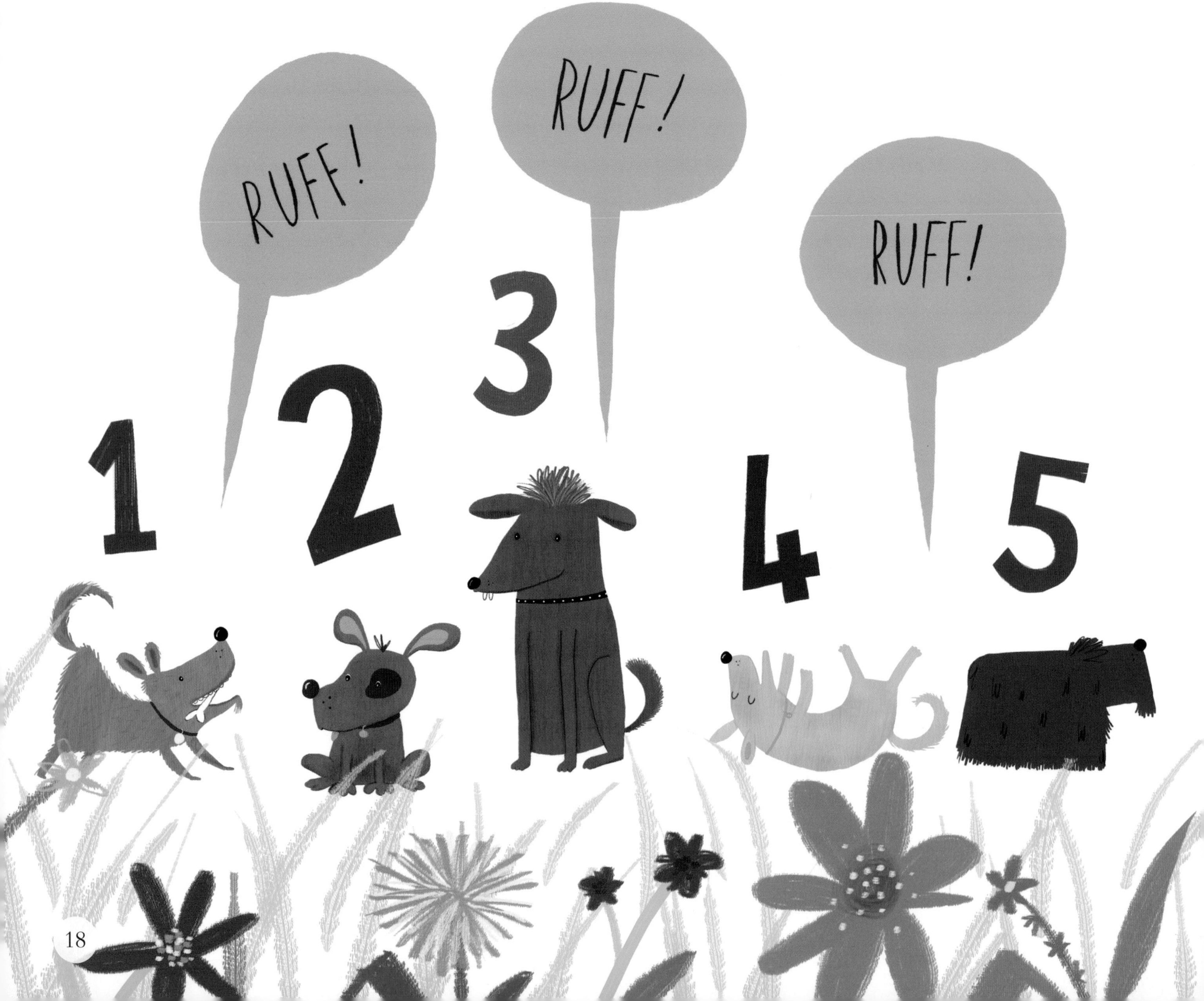
RUFF!
RUFF!
RUFF!
1
2
3
4
5

1 little, 2 little, 3 little puppies,
4 little, 5 little, 6 little puppies,
7 little, 8 little, 9 little puppies,
10 little puppies say, "Ruff, ruff, ruff."

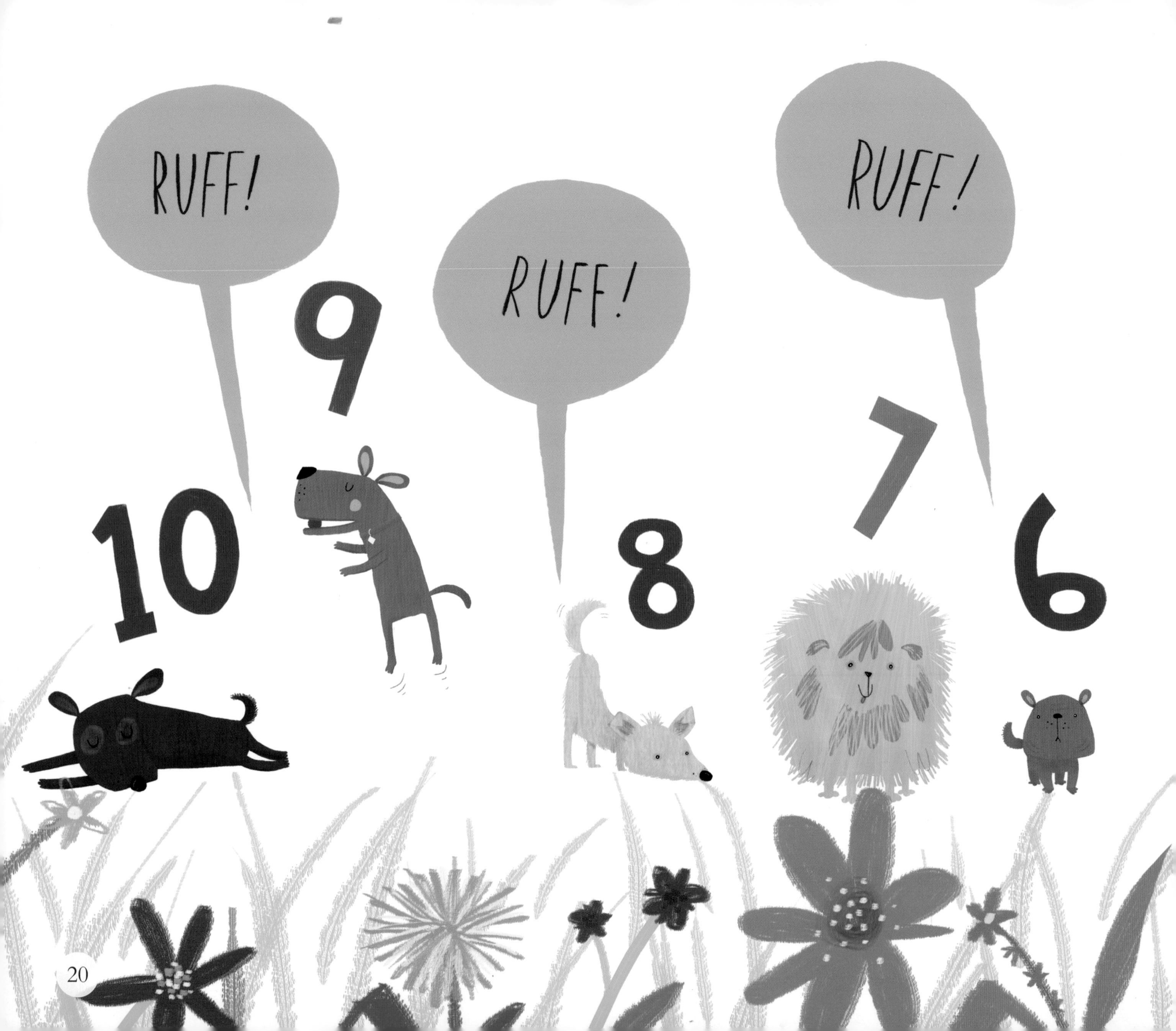
RUFF!
RUFF!
RUFF!
10
9
8
7
6

10 little, 9 little, 8 little puppies,
7 little, 6 little, 5 little puppies,
4 little, 3 little, 2 little puppies,
1 little puppy says, "Ruff, ruff, ruff."

GLOSSARY

chicks—baby chickens

piglets—baby pigs

trough—a long dish that holds food or water for pigs

10 Little Kittens

Public Domain

Traditional

TO LEARN MORE

Boynton, Sandra. *Doggies: A Counting and Barking Book*. New York: Little Simon Books, 1995.

Hines, Anna Grossnickle. *1, 2, Buckle My Shoe*. Orlando, FL: Harcourt, 2008.

Nunn, Daniel. *Counting 1 to 10*. Chicago: Raintree, 2012.

Pierce, Terry. *Counting Your Way: Number Nursery Rhymes*. Minneapolis: Picture Window Books, 2007.

Reasoner, Charles. *Hickory, Dickory, Dock*. North Mankato, MN: Picture Window Books, 2014.